to   Jacob

Simeon   Reuben   Leah   Rachel & Joseph   Jacob

Gad   Asher   Donkey   Sheep   Helper   Silver & Gold

To

From

HonorNet
P.O. Box 910
Sapulpa, Oklahoma 74067
www.honornet.net

Scripture taken from *THE MESSAGE*. Copyright © 1993, 1994, 1995, 1996, 2000, 2001, 2002. Used by permission of NavPress Publishing Group.

Jacob's Promise

A Story about Faith

Celia Banks

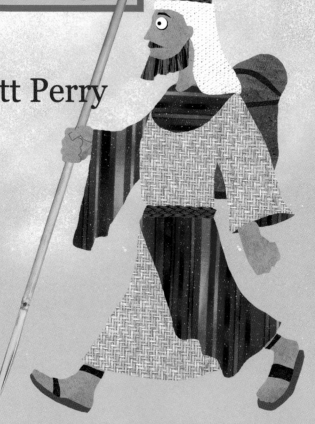

Illustrated by:
Janet Unalp and Matt Perry

Art directed by:
Celia Banks

Long ago and far away, a flock of sheep and goats lived in the desert.

Some of the sheep and goats were striped.
Some were spotted, and some were brown.
But most were white with soft fuzzy coats.
They played in the sand under the palm trees
all day.

They were the happiest animals in the desert.

The sheep and goats had a very special shepherd. His name was Jacob. Jacob watched over them with tender love and care. The sheep and goats were happy, but Jacob was sad.

Jacob was a long way from home. He had come to the desert to live with his Uncle Laban. Jacob took care of the sheep and goats, but their owner was Uncle Laban. Over the years, the flocks had grown, and Uncle Laban had become very rich.

JACOB'S HOMELAND

After all his hard work, Jacob still did not own even one little animal. How would he ever be able to go home without a flock of his own?

9

The animals knew that Jacob wanted to go back home.

"I don't get it," said one sheep. "Jacob has a nice life here. We all love him."

Another sheep said, "If the place he lived before was so great, why did he leave? Why does he want to go back?"

JACOB'S HOMELAND

"He wants to go home because God promised him the land," said a wise old goat. "He misses his home, and when he remembers God's promise to him, he is filled with a longing to go back."

"Promise? What is a promise?" asked a little lamb.

"A promise from God," the mama sheep said, "is when God says He is going to give something to you or do something for you.

"Jacob is holding on to the promise that came straight from God."

"What does it mean to hold on to a promise?" a soft little lamb asked. "Can you see a promise? How do you hold on to one?"

A mama sheep said, "It is like Jacob holding on to one of us when he carries us home sometimes. To hold on to a promise means to believe the promise in your heart and never let go of it, no matter what happens."

One of the little lambs asked, "Is Jacob going back with animals? Does that mean we're going too?"

"Yes," said a papa sheep. "That's what it means."

"What a trip that would be," said the little lamb. "I can just see it all now!"

17

"How is that going to happen?" said an old goat. "Greedy old Laban owns us. Jacob just takes care of us, and he's been tricked by Laban two times already."

"We will have to see what God does!" said a fuzzy mama sheep.

"It takes faith to hold on to a promise, and Jacob has faith. Jacob looks to God and what He can do. That is what faith is.

"Jacob believes it will happen, and Jacob knows God will give him a plan."

19

Not long after that, the sheep heard Jacob talking to Uncle Laban.

"I have worked for you a long time, and now I want to take my family and go back to my homeland," said Jacob.

"But I don't want you to leave. Stay here and I will pay you whatever you want," Uncle Laban said.

Jacob said, "No. I must go. I have worked hard, and your flocks have grown while I've been here. You can pay me by letting me take all of the striped and spotted and brown animals as my wages. From now on, every animal that is born striped, spotted, or brown will be mine. That way you will know that I haven't cheated you or stolen from you."

Uncle Laban agreed.

21

The animals all gathered together to discuss what they had just heard.

"There aren't very many of us striped, spotted, and brown sheep or goats," one of the animals said.

"Uncle Laban is trying to trick Jacob again," said another sheep. "He is always playing tricks on Jacob. Laban knows there won't ever be very many striped, spotted, and brown sheep. He thinks Jacob will never have enough sheep and goats to have his own flock."

"You're right!" said a mama sheep. "But God has given Jacob a promise and a PLAN!"

"Yes! God has given Jacob a plan," said a very wise mama sheep. "Jacob just sent most of the striped, spotted, and brown sheep and goats on a three-day journey. They went to a place far away from the rest of Laban's flock."

There in that faraway place, Jacob listened to God's plan and obeyed everything God told him to do.

First he gathered some sticks.

Then he peeled away part of the bark and made stripes and spots on the sticks.

Then he put the sticks in front of the water trough where the sheep and the goats came to drink.

"Why is Jacob putting those sticks with stripes and spots in front of our water trough?" one of the lambs asked.

The mama said, "Those sticks remind Jacob of God's promise. They help him believe what God told him and his grandfather Abraham."

"What did God promise Abraham?" a little goat asked.

"God told Abraham that he would have lots and lots of children and grandchildren and great-grandchildren..."

"How many?" asked the little goat.

"As many as the stars in the sky and the grains of sand in the desert," said a wise old mama goat.

"Wow," said the little goat. "That's a LOT."

31

Time passed.

Every day when the healthy, strong sheep and goats came to drink, Jacob put the sticks in front of the watering trough. The sheep began to fall in love and have baby sheep. The goats also began to fall in love and have baby goats.

In the spring, an amazing thing happened! There were lots and lots of healthy baby lambs and goats that had stripes, spots, and brown fuzzy coats.

"Look at all the striped, spotted, and brown sheep and goats," said a little baby sheep. "There are lots of them now!"

"Yes," said a papa sheep. "God's promise to Jacob has come true! Jacob held on to God's promise and God made it happen."

"Oh!" said a baby sheep, jumping up and down. "I get it! Knowing and believing God's promise is very important.

"That means it won't be long before Jacob leaves to go home. God's plan has really happened fast!

"Jacob had faith in God's promise, and look at what God did. There are soooooo many striped, spotted, and brown sheep and goats."

"Look," said one of the mama sheep. "Everybody is lining up with Jacob. They are getting ready to go to his homeland."

START HERE
Leaving for Jacob's Homeland

39

Jacob knew in his heart that what God had promised...God had done. Jacob had gone to Uncle Laban's as just one man with nothing. He returned to his homeland with twelve children and more animals and money and helpers than he could count in a day. God had made Jacob a wealthy man.

When Jacob arrived, his brother Esau said, "Welcome home!"

Jacob's Promise
A Story about Faith

is based on the following biblical account: Genesis 30:25-43; 31:3

After Rachel had had Joseph, Jacob spoke to Laban, "Let me go back home. Give me my wives and children for whom I've served you. You know how hard I've worked for you."

Laban said, "If you please, I have learned through divine inquiry that God has blessed me because of you." He went on, "So name your wages. I'll pay you."

Jacob replied, "You know well what my work has meant to you and how your livestock has flourished under my care. The little you had when I arrived has increased greatly; everything I did resulted in blessings for you. Isn't it about time that I do something for my own family?"

"So, what should I pay you?"

Jacob said, "You don't have to pay me a thing. But how about this? I will go back to pasture and care for your flocks. Go through your entire flock today and take out every speckled or spotted sheep, every dark-colored lamb, every spotted or speckled goat. They will be my wages. That way you can check on my honesty when you assess my wages. If you find any goat that's not speckled or spotted or a sheep that's not black, you will know that I stole it."

"Fair enough," said Laban. "It's a deal."

But that very day Laban removed all the mottled and spotted billy goats and all the speckled and spotted nanny-goats, every animal that had even a touch of white on it plus all the black sheep and placed them under the care of his sons. Then he put a three-day journey between himself and Jacob. Meanwhile Jacob went on tending what was left of Laban's flock.

But Jacob got fresh branches from poplar, almond, and plane trees and peeled the bark, leaving white stripes on them. He stuck the peeled branches in front of the watering troughs where the flocks came to drink. When the flocks were in heat, they came to drink and mated in front of the streaked branches. Then they gave birth to young that were streaked or spotted or speckled. Jacob placed the ewes before the dark-colored animals of Laban. That way he got distinctive flocks for himself which he didn't mix with Laban's flocks. And when the sturdier animals were mating, Jacob placed branches at the troughs in view of the animals so that they mated in front of the branches. But he wouldn't set up the branches before the feebler animals. That way the feeble animals went to Laban and the sturdy ones to Jacob.

The man got richer and richer, acquiring huge flocks, lots and lots of servants, not to mention camels and donkeys...

That's when God said to Jacob, "Go back home where you were born. I'll go with you."

DEDICATION

To my darling children Genevieve, Catherine, and John, who are gifts from God to me.

ACKNOWLEDGMENTS

This book is the result of a creative effort that involved many extremely talented people without whom this book would not have become a reality.

My thanks to Elizabeth Stuart, Kaley Stuart (age 10), Janice Ireland, Ron Callahan (my pastor), and the staff and members of my church, Grace Fellowship International.

OTHER BOOKS BY CELIA BANKS

ISSY'S GIFT
ISBN: 10: 0-9764460-7-3
ISBN: 13: 978-0-9764460-7-1

PROMISE OF HARVEST
ISBN: 10: 0-9764460-8-1
ISBN: 13: 978-0-9764460-8-8

Abraham

Isaac

God's Promise of Covenant

• God has made a promise, which He calls a covenant, to bless you and your children in spirit, soul, and body just as He blessed Abraham and Jacob. (3 John 2)

• God's covenant includes much more than forgiveness. It includes healing, deliverance, loving relationships, and everything else that is needed for a good life.

• God's covenant promises to provide believers with more than they need, so that they can share with others.

• God is the One who gives us the ability to create wealth...for the sake of His covenant. (Deuteronomy 8:18)

• God's promises are called God's Covenant. They are passed from generation to generation.
(Genesis 17:18; 26:3-4; 28:12-15)

What covenant promises has
God given to you and your family?

Jacob

God's Promise

Goat   Helper   Dinah   Zebulun   Issachar   Judah   Levi

Bilhah   Dan   Naphtali   Camel   Zilpah